WHEEDLE ON THE NEEDLE

written by: Stephen Cosgrove
illustrated by: Robin James

Printed in U.S.A.

ISBN #0-915396-04-1 WHEEDLE ON THE NEEDLE

P.O. Box 707
Bothell, Washington 98011

Dedicated to Seattle, Washington, a wonderfully warm place for a Wheedle to stay.

Many years ago, before anybody lived in the Northwest, there lived a very happy creature called a Wheedle. He was big, fat, and had a very large red nose. All day long he would play tag with the other animals of the forest or just sit around sniffing flowers.

One day while the Wheedle was playing, he happened to look down on the bay and saw a whole shipful of men arrive. They immediately set about building and clearing the ground. As they worked, they whistled. The more they worked, the more they whistled. And all that whistling noise hurt the poor Wheedle's ears, for he was very sensitive to whistling noises.

It was so bad that the Wheedle could get absolutely no sleep at all. Day by day he became grouchier and grouchier, to the point of grumbling at all his friends in the forest.

Finally the Wheedle decided he must put a stop to all that whistling. He thought for a moment and then realized that if all those men didn't have all their tools, they wouldn't be happy and therefore wouldn't whistle.

So that night he carefully stole all the tools. But the next morning the men quickly made new tools and started whistling all over again.

"Hmmmm," he grumbled. "What am I ever going to do to make those people quit making that whistling noise so I can get some sleep?" He decided that maybe the best thing to do was to scare them. Because when people are scared they can't pucker, and when they can't pucker, they can't whistle.

He began creeping up behind them and growling at the top of his voice. And sure enough, those men were so scared that they couldn't whistle. But one time he growled at a very brave lumberjack, and the lumberjack, to prove he wasn't scared, just whistled at the Wheedle.

Well, let me tell you, that just about scared the poor Wheedle to death. He jumped back, put his hands over his ears and ran into the forest.

It was then that the Wheedle knew he could no longer live near the bay. So he packed his belongings and moved away.

He wandered far and wide searching for some place that was far enough away from the men so he wouldn't have to listen to all that whistling and could get some sleep. He wandered farther into the forest until he came to the very top of Mount Rainier.

He listened very carefully. And as he couldn't hear even the faintest of whistles, he unpacked his sleeping bag, his toothbrush with the squiggly on the end, and his white woolly pajamas.

He quickly brushed his teeth, dressed in his pajamas, hopped in his sleeping bag and fell fast asleep.

He slept so hard that his big red nose went on and off just like a blinking light. But that didn't bother the Wheedle, and he slept and he slept. In fact he slept for many, many years undisturbed, high on Mount Rainier.

One day years and years later the Wheedle began to toss and turn in his sleep. Suddenly he woke with a start.

"What was that?" he grumbled as he rubbed the sleep from his eyes. He yawned once, stretched twice, and then peeked over the edge of the mountain to see what was going on.

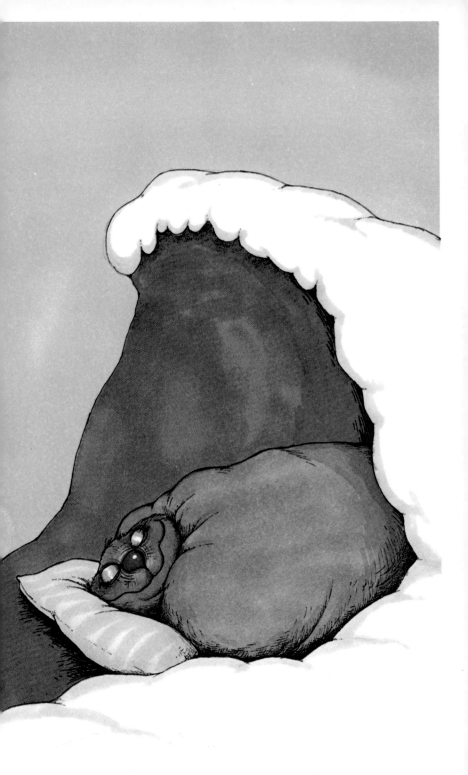

There, much to his surprise, he saw that the men had continued to build over the years, and now had built almost to the edge of the mountain. But what was more alarming than that was the fact that everybody was whistling.

"Oh, no!" cried the Wheedle. "What am I ever going to do now?"

"With all that noise I'll never get back to sleep," he grumbled.

The Wheedle began pacing up and down the mountain, mumbling and grumbling all the while. Then his eyes lit up and a smile crossed his lips. "I have it!" he growled. And with that he dug around in his possessions until he found the biggest sack he owned. Then he went to the very edge of the mountain, and by standing on his tiptoes he reached carefully into the sky and grabbed a cloud. Very gently he started stuffing clouds into the bag until he had it as full as he could get it.

With the bag thrown over his shoulder, he set out for the source of his noisy problem — Seattle.

When he finally arrived, he looked for the tallest building around in order to complete his plan. He picked, out of all the buildings, the Space Needle.

He carefully climbed to the top and gently laid down the bag of clouds. He looked all around and grumbled, "This wouldn't be such a bad place to live if it weren't for all that whistling." For you see, all around the Space Needle children were playing and the older people were working and they were all whistling.

The Wheedle reached into the bag, pulled out the biggest and wettest cloud, and threw it high into the sky. The cloud hung there for a moment, then began to rain on all the people below. Now people in Seattle like the rain and rainy days are fun, but it's very hard to whistle on rainy days because your lips get so wet.

"Ho, ho!" shouted the Wheedle. "Now I shall have some peace and quiet."

With the rain falling all around him, the Wheedle stretched out on top of the Space Needle and once again fell fast asleep.

Soon everybody in Seattle knew that the Wheedle was responsible for all the rain. And finally in desperation the mayor went to the top of the Space Needle to see if he could get the Wheedle to stop the rain, if only for a day, so that the people could whistle again. Very gently he shook the Wheedle by the shoulder. "Mr. Wheedle," he said, "please wake up."

The Wheedle rumbled and grumbled and finally woke up. "What is it!" he growled.

"Please," said the mayor, "could you stop making it rain? The people are becoming sadder and sadder because they can't whistle while they work."

The Wheedle then told the mayor his sad story. "I never meant to hurt or make anyone sad," he said. "But I just can't sleep with all that whistling going on."

The mayor thought for a moment. "I know what we shall do, Mr. Wheedle. I'll be back tomorrow morning with the answer to all our problems." With that he went back to town to set his plan in motion.

The mayor quickly called all the sailmakers in Seattle and had them bring all the cotton they could find to the Seattle Center.

Then, when they all arrived, they began sewing all that cotton together. They sewed pink cotton onto yellow cotton, and blue cotton onto red cotton, and by early morning they had finished the task.

Then all the people of Seattle, with the mayor at the lead, marched to the Space Needle and the sleeping Wheedle. They all stood around as the mayor once again woke the slumbering monster.

"Huh, what is it?" the Wheedle mumbled as he woke.

"Ahem," said the mayor as he cleared his throat. "Mr. Wheedle, as you can't sleep with all the whistling and all the people of Seattle are sad when they can't whistle, we hereby present you with these earmuffs so that you may sleep in peace." With that he gave the Wheedle the biggest, most colorful pair of earmuffs you have ever seen.

The Wheedle placed them over his ears and smiled for the first time in years.

The people were so happy, they began whistling with joy, but the Wheedle didn't mind because now he couldn't hear it. He slowly folded the bag of clouds and with the bag as a pillow, fell fast asleep. And he slept so soundly that once again his nose began to blink.

There's a Wheedle
On the Needle
I know just what
You're Thinking
But if you look up
Late at night
You'll see
His red nose blinking

BOOKS FROM SERENDIPITY

Written by Stephen Cosgrove

To order send cost of the books plus .25 postage and handling to:
Serendipity
P.O. Box 707
Bothell, Washington 98011

(Washington residents, please include sales tax of 5.4% with purchase.)